FIRST-GRADE FRIENDS

Our Funny
VALENTINE

by Judy Katschke
illustrated by Clare Elsom

Scholastic Inc.

ISBN 978-0-545-77605-9

Text copyright © 2015 by Judy Katschke
Illustrations copyright © 2015 by Clare Elsom

Published by Scholastic Inc. SCHOLASTIC and associated logos are trademarks and/or registered trademarks of Scholastic Inc.

10 9 8 7 6 5 4   17 18 19/0

Printed in the U.S.A.   40

First printing, February 2015

"Happy Valentine's Day!" Molly said.
She opened the door to Ms. Fickle's
classroom.
Heart balloons flew out.

There were more balloons inside.
Ms. Fickle was inside, too.

Ms. Fickle dressed up as someone
new every day.
Today she was the Queen of Hearts.
"Let's make valentines!" she said.

The kids began making valentines.
"Let's make one for Ms. Fickle,"
Colin said.
They cut out a big, red heart.
Then Kono cried, "Stop!"

"We have to make Ms. Fickle's valentine special," Kono said.
"But how?" asked Molly.
"I have an idea!" said Colin.

"Let's play ball with Ms. Fickle,"
Colin said.
"We can use our valentine as home
plate!"

Everyone liked Colin's idea.
Everyone but Kono.

"Ms. Fickle is the Queen of Hearts," Kono explained. "And queens don't play baseball."
"You're right, Kono," said Julia.
"We need another idea."

The kids thought and thought.
Then Josh said, "I have an idea!"

"Let's give our valentine some wings," Josh said. "We can fly around like a giant valentine bug!"

Everyone liked Josh's idea.
Everyone but Kono.

"I think bugs are gross," Kono said.
"What if Ms. Fickle thinks so, too?"
"You're right, Kono," said Andrew.
"We need another idea."

The kids thought and thought.
Then Julia said, "I have an idea!"

"Let's turn our valentine into a book!"
Julia said. "Ms. Fickle loves to read."

Everyone liked Julia's idea.
Everyone but Kono.

"Ms. Fickle has lots of books," Kono said. "What if she doesn't have time to read our valentine book?"
"You're right, Kono," said Colin. "We need another idea."

The kids thought and thought.
Then Molly said, "I have an idea!"

"Let's do a science project," Molly said. "We can make the valentine into a paper airplane!"

Everyone liked Molly's idea.
Everyone but Kono.

MOLLY'S FLYING POTION

"What if Ms. Fickle's plane flies out the window?" Kono said.
"You're right, Kono," said Josh.
"We need another idea."

The kids thought and thought.
Then Andrew said, "I have an
idea!"

"Let's paint on the card," Andrew said. "Then we can put it in a fancy frame for Ms. Fickle!"

Everyone liked Andrew's idea.
Everyone but Kono.

"What if paint gets all over the classroom?" Kono said. "And all over Ms. Fickle, too?"

"You're right, Kono," said Molly. "We need another idea."

Andrew, Colin, Josh, Julia, and Molly
had all shared their ideas.
And they had more ideas, too!

IDEAS:
HOME PLATE?
BUG WINGS?
BOOK?
AIRPLANE?
PAINTING?

The kids shouted out their ideas.
They tugged the big, red heart this
way and that.

Until—*RIIIIIIIP!*
The big, red heart ripped into pieces!

"Oh, no!" Kono said.

Now they had <u>no</u> valentine for their teacher!

Just then, Ms. Fickle came back in.

"Cool! A Valentine's Day puzzle!"
Ms. Fickle said.
Kono looked at the pieces of the
valentine and smiled.
"Yes! We made it together."

"This is the most special Valentine's Day ever!" Ms. Fickle said.
The kids had a great Valentine's Day, too—because they had a special teacher, Ms. Fickle!